Bye-bye, Turtle!

T0337180

Written by Katie Foufouti
Illustrated by Deborah Partington

Collins

Who and what is in this story?

Listen and say 🎧①

beach

Download the audio at www.collins.co.uk/839774

Julia

pedal boat

Pedal boats

Julia's mum

🎧 ② Julia is at the beach with her family.

Julia loves the beach, but today she doesn't want to swim.

Pedal boats

She wants to try a pedal boat.

Look at those boats!

Pedal boats

Julia and her mum are on a pedal boat in the sea.

From the boat, they can see beautiful, small fish.

Julia can jump in the sea.

Julia can swim to the rock.

Julia is on the rock. She is looking at the sea.

What can you see?

Julia says, "Is it a big fish?
Is it an old bag?"

Julia is on the pedal boat again.

Let's go and see!

It's a turtle in a bag.

The turtle isn't swimming. The turtle is sad.

It's in a bag and it can't swim.

Julia's mum swims to the turtle.
She wants to help it.

Mum finds a shell and cuts the bag.

The turtle can swim now!

Picture dictionary

Listen and repeat

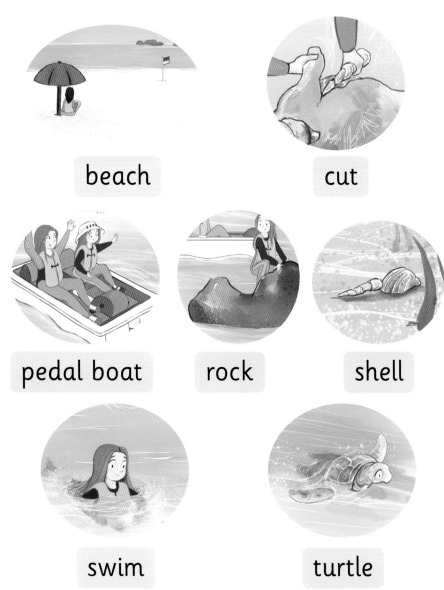

beach

cut

pedal boat

rock

shell

swim

turtle

1 Look and order the story

2 Listen and say

Collins

Published by Collins
An imprint of HarperCollins*Publishers*
Westerhill Road
Bishopbriggs
Glasgow
G64 2QT

HarperCollins*Publishers*
1st Floor, Watermarque Building
Ringsend Road
Dublin 4
Ireland

William Collins' dream of knowledge for all began with the publication of his first book in 1819.

A self-educated mill worker, he not only enriched millions of lives, but also founded a flourishing publishing house. Today, staying true to this spirit, Collins books are packed with inspiration, innovation and practical expertise. They place you at the centre of a world of possibility and give you exactly what you need to explore it.

© HarperCollins*Publishers* Limited 2020

10 9 8 7 6 5 4 3 2

ISBN 978-0-00-839774-6

www.collins.co.uk/elt

British Library Cataloguing in Publication Data

A catalogue record for this publication is available from the British Library.

Author: Katie Foufouti
Illustrator: Deborah Partington (Beehive)
Series editor: Rebecca Adlard
Commissioning editor: Fiona Undrill
Publishing manager: Lisa Todd
Product managers: Jennifer Hall and Caroline Green
In-house editor: Alma Puts Keren
Project manager: Emily Hooton
Editor: Tessie Papadopoulou-Dalton
Proofreaders: Natalie Murray and Michael Lamb
Cover designer: Kevin Robbins
Typesetter: 2Hoots Publishing Services Ltd
Audio produced by id audio, London
Reading guide author: Emma Wilkinson
Production controller: Rachel Weaver
Printed and bound by: GPS Group, Slovenia

Download the audio for this book and a reading guide for parents and teachers at www.collins.co.uk/839774